Alfred Welch

Extracts from the Diary of Moritz Svengali

Alfred Welch

Extracts from the Diary of Moritz Svengali

ISBN/EAN: 9783337197001

Printed in Europe, USA, Canada, Australia, Japan

Cover: Foto ©Raphael Reischuk / pixelio.de

More available books at **www.hansebooks.com**

EXTRACTS FROM THE DIARY OF MORITZ SVENGALI

Translated and Edited by Alfred Welch

Be just to all mankind, my friend ;
They seek the same as you ;
Their different manners but depend
On chance and point of view.

NEW YORK
HENRY HOLT AND COMPANY
1897

PREFACE.

THE following pages have been selected from the private diary of the famous master, Moritz Svengali, which, upon his death, came into the possession of his aunt Marta Adler, and was intrusted by her to the editor with many tearful injunctions as to the care with which the precious memento was to be preserved.

As is well known, this incomparable musician died suddenly at Drury Lane Theater just as he and Mme. Svengali were about to begin their series of concerts, which, in the season of 185-, the London public had so eagerly anticipated.

It will be remembered that Svengali
was too ill to conduct the concert as
usual on what was to be the opening
night; but took his place in one of the
boxes from which he could easily be
seen by his wife, who was so devoted to
him that she never sang except in his
presence.

No one who, on that memorable night,
breathlessly awaited the first notes of
her marvelous voice, will forget the
disappointment of the audience when
Mme. Svengali broke down immediately upon her appearance, nor the hor-
ror and sympathy that succeeded when
it was discovered that the cause of her
failure was that, on glancing toward her
husband's box, instead of meeting his
look of encouragement, she saw his life-
less body leaning against the rail.

It is probably unnecessary to say that

the whole diary is not given; but only such parts as throw light upon the most interesting portions of the life of this remarkable man and best serve to illustrate his character and genius. Some portions would be of no interest to the public, others are devoted to private family matters, and other pages, apparently written under the influence of passion, are very disconnected and have many lines crossed out; as if the writer had, in a calmer mood, repented of his anger.

As it is almost impossible to paraphrase in English many of the idioms of the Polish Hebrew dialect, it has been thought best to abandon all attempts to preserve the peculiarities of the author's style or the forms of expression of his native tongue, in which the diary is written.

THE DIARY OF
MORITZ SVENGALI.

February 5th, 185–.

To-morrow I leave for Paris. It is good to turn one's back upon the old life of Porlisz. Yes, and even upon that of Vienna and Leipsic. The shadow of the Ghetto is over them all, for me, and the smell of the long, narrow streets with their overhanging gables, that shut out what little light might come down but for them.

If the mother and the sisters and all the others were but away, I should never again travel the road I am to take; after I am once gone, no matter whither the way ahead might lead, I would go on and on, further and further away from all the dark and dingy cities and the more gross and brutal provinces, with their stupid prejudices and their ridiculous grandees and their contemptuous petty officials, clanking their swords and jingling their spurs, and insulting for very wantonness every Jew who walks upright in their presence.   Oh! if only I could come back and trample upon them all—and, if not, never come back at all; but send for the mother and the rest to live in some more friendly region, if there is such, where at least one need not cringe to escape insult.

February 6th.

WHEN the train passes the curve beyond the river, I shall see the last of
Porlisz. Not perhaps the last of the
church spires and the towers of the
public buildings—those you can see until
they are hidden by the hills; but of the
Porlisz that I have known—the group of
low houses between the cemetery and
the marshy land near the river, where
there is nothing to break the dull monot-
ony of the dark roofs. Truly I never
realized until now the advantages of hav-
ing a birthplace it is so easy to leave.
Even from this distance, where one cannot perceive the dirt and squalor, it is
not hard to say farewell. One travels
very lightly when he has not even regrets

to bind him to his old home.   As for me, all that I leave has been repulsive and degrading; only my music has been my inspiration, and that I carry with me, to Paris, to London, to America if I will; wherever I wish to travel.   Already the old life seems far away.   I wonder if it is in truth all left behind, or shall I awake and find it with me yet?

The coach is so full that I can scarcely move my hand to write.   The one in front contains Baron von Modlin and his brother, no others.   I was about to take one of the vacant seats, when the guard slammed the door and ordered me to crowd into this place where all the seats were already filled, and Frau Roepell had to take her child upon her lap to make room for me.

.   .   .   .   .

We have just changed for the train on the main' line.   I was a little ahead of the others, and was the first to enter an empty coach. Baron von Modlin and his brother have been hurried into the seats opposite me. They have been complaining bitterly to one another that a coach was not kept free for them, as at Porlisz. It seems that the places they wished to secure were reserved for Count Chelm. Ah, my friends! you should not have passed beyond the bounds of your province if you wished to preserve the flattering consideration accorded to local magnates. My little flageolet here in my coat pocket may yet prove a better claim to recognition than your tumble-down schloss on the hill above Porlisz. After all, it is a matter of perspective. The schloss doubtless seems much smaller viewed from Paris, than when one looks up from the streets of the Judenstrasse.

March 18th.

AND this is Paris, the dream of my life. No, not the dream. How could I dream of this in Porlisz? But this is the realization of all my fancies—my ideals—the thing I longed for and could not tell. It is good, so good that I cannot yet credit it, to be away from the old life. The mother was dear, and Marta and the rest; but, oh! the narrow walls and the sordidness, and worse than all, the contempt—the scorn—the indignities—always—always!

Here the people are courteous, even if they are strangers and careless. To-day I spoke to a man on the Boulevard. I asked him the way to the Rue Castiglione. He was a professional or an official, by his appearance. I almost knew the way, but stopped him because he looked friendly—and so he was. He answered me with as much consideration as though I were M. le Maire or a friend of his, which I was for the moment; and he touched his hat.

The day before I left Porlisz, I spoke to Franz Fredro, the steward of the Radinski estates. I told him of some changes which were needed in the house we occupied on the estate lands, and tried to arrange that they should be made when I was gone. He answered contemptuously, and shouted "Get out of my way!" and the dirt thrown back from his horse's feet covered me as he almost rode me down before I could stand aside. But he is a swine and a boor—a servant of an excellency, and knows nothing of manners, and, I hope, will never know Paris.

March 23d.

THIS has been a red-letter day for me. I was beginning to feel a little alone among all the life and stir about me, especially as I have not yet found any opportunity to have myself heard, when I met Gecko—Gecko, just the same as when I first found him playing for copper coins on the streets of Vienna, only better dressed and not so thin. I have not seen him since he left us there, and did not know he had come to Paris. He is playing at the Gymnase, and plays much better than he did. I am to give him some more lessons, and we will play together. It is good to meet a friend again—yes, even if he is part of the old despised provincial life. He lodges in the Impasse des Ramoneurs, and I have found lodgings not far off, in the Rue Tire-Liard. I must not spend so much, and must find an engagement very soon. I have not been able as yet to settle down to real life here, and what I brought with me is almost gone. Well—it is the reaction after what I have left. Soon the dazzle will be gone, and my eyes will become accustomed to the brighter light. I wonder how it would seem to be here free from all thought of the morrow, like the students I saw dancing last Sunday in the garden at "la loge du garde Champêtre." I also wonder if the dancing keeps up when they are no longer students, and have families to look after like other men, and perhaps less to do it with. If not, they are all the more wise to do their dancing now. If they learn the step, they may be able to keep it up even after the music stops.

March 28th.

I AM never done walking the streets, upright, with none to scoff and insult me because I do not cringe and make salutes where none will be returned by the mighty little grandees who expect them as their due—dogs who have nothing but their evil envy of genius, and the power to taunt those who know more than they ever dreamed. There are aristocrats and excellencies here—yes; but they are not so near to one as at Porlisz nor even at Vienna or Frankfort, and therefore not so offensive; or perhaps they are too busy and interested in their own lives to go out of their way to worry; besides, I think they are of a better spirit.

I have met a comfortable Englishman. Not exactly an Englishman; but one, I think, of the Scotland part. He is not arrogant nor supercilious, although somewhat abrupt, but I have learned that this is with them often merely a cover to hide their lack of polish, and means nothing unkind underneath. I was playing in the Jardin Bullier. I told Gecko I had spent all my money, and he found me an engagement through his acquaintance with the leader of the orchestra. There was a member ill, and so I took his place. I was faint when it was over, for I had waited for something to eat until I had my pay. Another of the company introduced me to the Englishman, as he stood near our table. The man who introduced me to him will take me to his studio to-morrow. He is an artist. His name is McAllister. He has his studio with two friends—real Englishmen—who walked away with him.

March 30th.

I HAVE been to the studio of the Scotch-Englishman. He was there with his two friends. Their studio is in the Place St. Anatole des Arts, and is large and fine for a studio in the Latin Quarter—very different indeed from some. It is light and high, not low and mean like my den in the Rue Tire-Liard. There is room to move and live, and they have a piano. They are much more courteous than most English—almost, sometimes, like the French; but then too, they are a little like the Germans and only see the good of their own. Perhaps it is well to be content with one's own ways and belongings, if one is not so well satisfied that he can learn nothing new.

April 7th.

WHY have those three artists so much that they know not how to use, and I so little? Even Gecko could do better. Some day I too will have, and then I will show them how I hate their self-satisfied ways and their taking everything for granted that they should have it, while I—I have to work hard for every little advance; and, when I have accomplished, I am despised. Why will they not treat me also as one of themselves? To-day Gecko and I went to their studio in the Place St. Anatole des Arts. I went to take Gecko, who wished to visit it and to play upon their piano. We found them all at work, but not too busy to hear Chopin, and so we gave them something that I do not believe they had even in their own homes which they seem to so strangely regret. While we played, a girl entered. She was a model for Durien, a sculptor in the same building. She was an English girl and most beautiful. Such as I have never seen before. I wonder if all English girls are like that. And yet they say she is not altogether English either. It seems that the English is a good stock on which to graft some other stock. A little Scotch or Irish or almost any other strain wonderfully improves the individual. The girl's name is Trilby—Trilby O'Ferrall. She is tall and straight and slender, and her voice—I cannot describe it. It is like an organ, clear and rich and strong. But when she sings—she thinks she can sing—oh, but she makes horrible work! She does not know that there are even two notes.

After she had gone, one of the English-men, the smallest, whom they call "Little Billee" (the third is very tall and strong and they call him "Taffy"), the little one played for us the air that the girl had tried to sing—they call it "Ben Bolt"—and Gecko and I played it afterward. It is a simple melody—a plain folk song.

I must see that girl and hear her speak again. Her voice is a grand instrument in the house of a bourgeois who knows nothing of music. If only I had that voice instead of my poor little flageolet, which has been more than ever inade-quate for me since I have heard her speak!

April 20th.

I HAVE been again to the Place St.
Anatole des Arts.   The Scotch-Englishman would be quite companionable but
for his friends.   The English girl was
there again, and she loves the little
artist.   I could see it almost from the
first.   They are at heart aristocrats or,
what is much worse, worshipers of the
aristocrats, and have all, and I nothing.
She does not understand music, which is
the only means .I have of expressing
myself, and so I am shut off and must
stand by and see them enjoy all her company and attention.   They do not understand music either, and she spends her
time with them while I could play with
her voice like on a flute, and she will npt

attend to me when the little artist is near to look upon. To-day, in play, I seized him by the arms and held him until the large man—Taffy—pinned my arms to my side and almost crushed the bones. I cannot play to-night. I have no patience to stand anything when I think of that girl's voice and of her. Honorine, whom I have been teaching, I can no longer tolerate—to-day I sent her away.

May 1st.

To-day I have seen the mysteries of an Englishman's bath—two of them. I came this morning in upon both Little Billee and Taffy as they were trying to get themselves clean—their daily practice as I am told. It is a habit that requires opportunity. I wonder how they would pursue it in the residences of the Judenstrasse. That is not a good source from which to inherit the fashion of playing with soap and water daily. I "chaffed" them, as my Englishmen call it, and laughed at them; but, ah, messieurs—your Bohemia is very far from the real land. It is only in the provinces. And then again, Bohemia is very far from the land of despair, which is beyond all the countries known to your geographers; and it is a long, long journey from that land through all the provinces of Bohemia to the land of success, where I mean to live some day.

.   .   .   .   .

Last night everything seemed against me. To-day I have hope. It all came suddenly and by accident. I was on my way to the studio in the Place St. Anatole des Arts, and met the English girl coming down the stairs and crying with pain in her head. I made her sit down in the studio, and soon charmed away her pain with a few simple passes. It is easy with her, for she is docile and a good subject. Even Little Billee could not make her look at him when she is in that sleep. Then she is mine—all mine; and all the little Englishmen and the big Englishmen cannot take her from me.

I do not know whether it is her voice or herself that has spoiled my taste for all other music. If I find her with the pain in her head again, she will be mine until she is well and, perhaps, who knows—she may come to think of me and not of the little artist.

September 11th.

I HAVE seen Trilby again to-day. If she would only look at me as she does at Little Billee; if she would only be ill again so that I might charm away the pain! I do not know why I want the pain to come again now. Is it so that I may have a chance to help her, or to take her away from him ?

There is a painting I saw to-day in a shop window near the Boulevard des Italiens. It is entitled "In Love and War, all is fair." Claude Bertholet, who was with the English army in the East, says it is one of their sayings, and is their excuse for anything they may desire to do when they have the power.

I wonder if it is not all fair for me also—In love and war ?—I would not have doubted if it had been Honorine; but with her—it is different.

October 1st.

THERE is a reward for waiting. I have tasted some of the sweets of success, and they pay for years of work. Last night was the night of my concert. I have already played at two or three grand concerts with Gecko; but last night was my own. The audience did not care whence I came, nor who I was, but every number was encored, and the last again and again. This is what I have imagined and dreamed of. I am to repeat it next week.

In the fourth row to the right was Baron von Modlin. Of course he did not know me. He was introduced to me after the concert was over. He said he understood I was from Poland, and

that he also was from that country. I
asked him from what town, and he said
from Porlisz. I did not tell him I was
quite familiar with the aspect of the
schloss from the window of my attic in
the Judenstrasse. We did not, however,
dine together at Porlisz, as we did last
night at Durand's.

Besides the applause, there is the
tangible reward of money enough and to
spare in one's pocket. That is not perhaps so intoxicating at the moment; but
it lasts over to the next day. I have
fitted myself out from head to foot and
will visit our friends in the Place St.
Anatole des Arts. Ah—this is life, to
walk down the Boulevard on such a
morning, with the memory of success in
one's mind and the tribute of genius in
one's pocket. I wonder how many of
those who pass know what it means to

walk upright, instead of cringing along in the memory of the days when the public promenades were forbidden to one's race; and how sweet the tradition of the "Wheel" (that it takes more than one generation to forget) makes it to dress as one pleases.

October 10th.

WHEN I see Trilby and find her so engrossed in the little artist, all my good will and happiness vanish, and I say things that it fills me with shame and disgust to remember. I am eaten up with jealousy, and cannot control my tongue.

December 25th.

LAST night I met Gecko at the Gymnase, and after our engagements were
over, we strolled together across the
Place de la Concorde and at last up the
Rue de la Madeleine. We were occupied
with the fine night, and the holiday
throng and all the stir of Paris around
us, so that we did not notice which way
we went until we were already almost
upon the steps of the Madeleine itself.
The crowd almost carried us into the
building before we had time to draw
back. Our three friends of the Place St.
Anatole des Arts passed us and entered
the church. Gecko and I stood back in
a recess near the door until the people
should pass sufficiently to allow us to

return.   Before we could force our way
against the crowd, the great organ be-
gan.   Gecko was spell-bound.   I found
he did not wish to leave.   Indeed he
would have entered the church if I had
consented, but I did not wish to be seen
there, especially by our English friends.
So we waited in the little recess just outside the door, well out of the way of
notice, until the organ ceased, and then
we walked away.   The street was very
quiet now, for all were in the church;
and we were silent too.   And, as the
night was cold, although bright, we
went to my lodgings and played together
until long after midnight.   Gecko tried
to recall some themes we had heard
from the organ, and I supplied what I
could remember, but it was not "Il bel
canto."

December 26th.

THIS is a different atmosphere and a very different life from that of Porlisz. I never thought I should escape far enough from the shadow of the barred gates of the "Street" to attend a Christmas festival. Yet that is how I spent last night. The further a man wanders from the boundaries of his early prejudices, the more he wishes to explore. I wish I knew how to wholly break down the barriers between the studio in the Place St. Anatole des Arts and myself. If it were not for Trilby, and her fondness for the little artist that angers me so, it would be easier.

Last night I saw the three Englishmen at their best. They had invited, beside myself, Durien the sculptor from their own house, and Vincent the young American student, and Dodor and Zouzou, two young soldiers, and Antony, a Swiss, and others whom I did not know. Gecko was with me. Our welcome was hearty, and all the spirit of the evening was kind and good. I came nearer to those men than ever before—nearer than to any men. We were all good comrades, and all the strife of different races and of art and ambition (except so that it might amuse us) was left outside the studio door. I wonder how much of this life there is in the world beyond what I have seen. That is what one does not always discover by travel. No—I will not comment. The boys were young; it was their Christmas night and a festival, and the wine was good and they had welcomed Gecko and myself as brothers, and that is much—is everything to one who has heard through his father's tales the "Hep—Hep" of the mob in the streets. Trilby and her friend Mme. Angèle Boisse and Mme. Vinard served the tables. Ah, Trilby! Trilby! I would give all my life and my years of toil at music if you would but look on me as you looked on Little Billee last night. And yet, I know not how it was, but in their company, amid the good fellowship of the evening, I was not able to remember my anger against him, and to-day it is all sorrow. I wish I had never met Trilby at the studio. I wish I had lived and died in the slime of the Ghetto, and never known that there was any life outside of Porlisz. That is the misery of catching a glimpse of the bright side of life, when one has always lived in its shadow.   The after days are more bitter and lonely by the contrast.   But, oh—if I had only known the possibilities of life before it was too late!   If only some one little surrounding had drawn up, and not all—all crushed down; so that all— every attempt to rise, must come from within, except what little the father and mother could do, and they had so little of courage or strength left to give, after their own struggles—then—then—I too might have been erect and clear-eyed and resolute, and had the bearing to attract, instead of only the art that speaks for itself but not—not always for the artist.

One thing I have resolved.   I will not charm Trilby to follow me if she loves Little Billee.   It is sweet to hold her even for a moment under my power, so that she may think and speak only what

I will. It is my only advantage; but I will give it up. It shall be a fair fight. He is young, he is graceful and smooth-cheeked and has the carriage of an aristocrat. It cannot be expected that the eyes of a girl should look beyond the wrinkles and scars of years, and see what might have been if the struggle had been less fierce.

The little fellow was excited with wine last night, but in very good spirits. We boxed, and he planted a blow straight in my face before I could ward him off. I was trying to parry his passes without hurt to him. He was too flushed to really spar in earnest. Afterward, I watched him as he started for his lodgings in the Place de l'Odéon. I fear he had some little difficulty in making his way home; but, as Dodor and Zouzou were with him, I thought one of them would be sober enough to pilot the others.

I will go back to my own province of music. There I am at home. It is a democracy where all have an equal chance.

January 5th, 185–.

THERE is trouble at the studio in the Place St. Anatole des Arts; and Trilby has gone. Where, I do not know. I met Dodor. He first told me. I went to see her friend Mme. Angèle Boisse in the Rue des Cloîtres Ste. Pétronille. She was not at home. I was in terror of what might have happened to Trilby. I had made myself resigned if she loved Little Billee and not me, if he would care for her and love her as I would; but not to let her lose herself like this! I went to the studio, and found that Little Billee was sick in bed. Two ladies, his mother and his sister, were nursing him. I talked to Taffy and the Scotch-Englishman. They knew nothing of where Trilby had gone, and had done nothing to find her. They said she wished to go away and be forgotten. Would they do so if she were one of their own—if she were the sister? I learned from Mme. Vinard that there had been a terrible quarrel, and that the mother and sister and a queer little man, a priest, his uncle, came to prevent the marriage of Little Billee to Trilby. It is as if she had been a plaything—a fancy—and now, they are tired, or she is in the way, and so they let her go. Anywhere—wherever she will. Is their life so full over there that they can neglect such as she?

I could not answer what I thought. He was ill, and the ladies were tending him; and the others seemed to be thinking only of him. Now I will find her; and if I do, she shall be mine—all mine;

and I will never again think that I must give her up if I can keep her in any way whatever—not to those who count matters of convenience of so much importance, and her of so little value.

January 10th.

I HAVE spent all my time for days searching for Trilby. It is not to be supposed that a girl would know where to go far when she is in so much trouble. She has taken her brother, little Jeannot, with her. I do not know whether Mme. Angèle Boisse or Mme. Vinard know where she has gone. If either of them does know, she refuses to tell.

February 1st.

I HAVE looked for Trilby for days and days—all the time I have free to myself, especially on the other side of the City, as I have thought she might hide there. Sometimes I have visited the Morgue and thought, with disgust of myself, how, in the madness of my jealousy, I talked to her of this. Each time I have gone there, I have had to force myself to enter, for fear of what I might find. This morning I walked through the streets on the other side of the Seine as long as I was able. The day was fine; but it has been all one to me for weeks past. This evening again, before I kept my engagement with Gecko, I walked up and down all the streets on my way.

All places are seven times as far by my way as by the straight path. I passed other men at dusk, going to their homes where their wives awaited them. I wonder if they guessed what envious eyes watched them as they hurried along. If Trilby would wait for me some day, I would forgive all the hardships of my life that is past. I would be satisfied, even if it were but for a few years.

February 5th.

MME. BOISSE has, at last, acknowledged that she knows where Trilby is. She is at Vibraye. I have written her and will write again in a day or two; and will go and fetch her as soon as she will come away.

February 20th.

TRULY, as the mother said, "It is good that a man should both hope and wait patiently."

Three nights ago I played at a concert which Gecko and I had arranged with two or three other friends. It was late when I reached my lodgings, and I threw myself on my bed, too tired to write again that night. I had hoped for a letter from Trilby by this time; but there was none. So I fell asleep, wondering whether she might not have come back to the studio, and planning to call there in the morning and inquire. It must have been near morning when I was awakened by a knock at my door; and, when I opened it, there, on the threshold, stood Trilby. It all seemed so natural—as though there could have

been no other end to my search. She
was disguised in man's clothing, and
was very weak and hungry. She had
been to my old lodging in the Rue Tire-
Liard, and from there had followed me
to the Rue des Saints Pères. I found
her some bread and butter and coffee,
and she ate and drank ravenously—and
then she slept—slept for two days and
two nights; while I watched and waited
for her to wake, and Gecko took my
place or found someone—I know not
whom—to do it for me when I should
have played. I care not whether my
place was filled at all or not, for now she
is mine—wholly mine. It is to me she
has come, and not to the Place St.
Anatole des Arts; and I did not charm
her or draw her to me in any way, but
she came of her own free will; and they
can never take her away from me again.

February 23d.

TRILBY has rested herself and is stronger, although still very weak. She has told me of her meeting with Mme. Bagot, Little Billee's mother, and of what passed between them and of all her wanderings. I was right. She did love Little Billee, and would have married him but for his mother coming and persuading her. She seems to have no bitterness; but only to be very grieved and yet tender in her feelings toward them all. I would want to kill; but she is an angel. She says she would never have come back to Paris had not her little brother died at Vibraye; and she, poor girl! was almost crazed with grief.

He was all she had left to her. So she wandered back to Paris in a man's dress, so that she should be safer from interference; and when she reached here, knew not where else to go, and finally came to me. When she is sufficiently well and strong, we will leave Paris and go to Germany; or, perhaps, even back to Porlisz; away from all thought of the studio in the Place St. Anatole des Arts; and there she will forget and grow happy and light-hearted again. And I—I am happy every day and every hour when she is near me. I did not know there was so much happiness in the world. When I go out, I am anxious until I come back, and hurry in to be sure it is all true and she is still there. Was this what all those men knew whom I saw hastening home at evening when I was searching for Trilby? I do not wonder they walked quickly and eagerly; I too hasten to reach our home, like other men, now that she is there, waiting for me.

March 2d.

To-day we saw Paris fade away behind us. The Paris that I so long desired in vain to see, and, when I saw it, found to exceed my highest expectations. And yet I am glad to see it disappear, for I am taking with me Trilby, the best reward of my sojourn there. Her spirits rose as we got away from the city and into the fields beyond; and by the time the last glimpse had disappeared, she seemed almost like her old self. It is the shadow of the old life, and the haunting memory of the studio in the Place St. Anatole des Arts, she is escaping, and I think she is anxious to blot them all out. I will see to it very carefully that nothing reminds her of her three artist friends. It is not well for either of us that those memories should be revived. She has told me much of her old life and of her father and mother. Her mother was a bar-maid at the Montagnards Écossais in the Rue du Paradis Poissonnière; and her father was an English clerical, who drank and gambled and lost his standing. Dodor, who was at school in England, tells me that there seems to be an inexplicable tendency among Englishmen of that class to marry barmaids, if they can only free themselves from their social prejudices sufficiently to do so. Her mother's father was also an aristocrat—the Honorable Colonel Desmond. He deserted Trilby's grandmother, and left her to shift for herself and his daughter, then a little child. Under the circumstances, I am not surprised that Trilby did not return to the studio.

I am going back to the places I have hated; but that is nothing. I can visit them with indifference now. Trilby is with me, and all else counts for nothing. Two can bear with courage and even laughter what would crush the spirit of one alone. Besides, I have learned that Porlisz, and even Vienna and Warsaw, are not all the world. Provincial grandees cannot hurt one who is freed from their influence by a taste of the broader life of Paris. I can afford to smile at their childish airs and pretenses. They may be amusing or even, sometimes, annoying; but they cannot overawe.

March 25th.

TRILBY gains every day. She is amused, and her thoughts are distracted from herself by the novelty of the life about her; she is trying to pick up some of the language. Gecko has joined us. He is to rest and to see his people before he goes back to Paris.

April 30th.

ALL who hear Trilby speak say it is so unfortunate that she cannot sing. Many will not believe that it is impossible. I cannot let her even attempt it for them; it would only expose her to ridicule, since she does not appreciate her own inability. I have tried to teach her; but she cannot distinguish one note from another. I thought, in Paris, that perhaps it was lack of opportunity; but no —it is fundamental. She can never learn.

May 15th.

GECKO was with us again to-day on his
way back to Paris.   He has made a sug-
gestion; or rather it came to us both.
We were speaking of Trilby's voice—how
it is like a great organ with no one to
play upon it; but every now and then,
when she speaks, it is as if a child came
and touched a note, and one longs to
hear it in the hands of a master.   He
urged me to try once more to teach her
to sing at least simple melodies; but I
told him how hopeless it was, and how
she tried to please me but could not
understand wherein she came short, and
so fretted over it and thought me un-
reasonable and cruel.   He reminded me
how I brought Fredro, a fellow-student

at Leipsic, so under my influence by a
few passes that he followed the move-
ment of my hand upon the keyboard and
actually struck several notes in succes-
sion correctly. . . I am to try if I cannot control Trilby's voice through my
own will while she is under my influence,
so that I may sing through her lips.
Perhaps, in time, I can so train her
voice that she may come to understand
and really sing herself.

May 16th.

IT can be done; at least to some extent. How much of practical result we may be able to accomplish remains to be seen. Gecko will not return to Paris immediately; but will stay with us for a time at least. He is most sanguine of success—more so than I am myself. I do not know whether he is more enthusiastic as a musician or as an admirer of Trilby, whom he is impatient to see upon the platform. He does not remember that she will be unconscious of her triumph, even if we succeed, and that she does not value musical achievement as we do.

December 15th, 185–.

TO-DAY Trilby made her first appearance in public. What she sang, she has rehearsed with me over and over again. How often she does not know herself. The success was beyond all that we had dared to hope. The audience was actually frantic with enthusiasm. Men and women wept with delight. Again and again they thronged to the platform and begged for but one more song. Some tore off their jewels and threw them at her feet. Now she sleeps. She has borne the strain of the constant practice well. I will watch until she wakes; for I am anxious to know whether the singing is too much for her. If she is strong enough, we will go to Vienna after a few more concerts in the smaller towns, and then on to St. Petersburg.

October 2d, 185-.

To-morrow we leave for Paris. It is almost five years since we traveled that road. They have been years of labor and anxiety and, at last, of triumph. There is no limit to the admiration and applause that greet Trilby wherever she appears. Warsaw, Vienna, St. Petersburg—all the eastern cities. We have thoroughly tested her powers; and her fame has preceded her to Paris.

October 5th.

TRILBY and I are at the Hôtel Bertrand. Our return to Paris has been quite different from our departure. Now her name is everywhere, and she is just the same as when she stole through the streets disguised as a boy, to escape observation. No—I hope not just the same. She still speaks of the little artist; but I have lately thought that the remembrance was growing dim. Sometimes I fear that it was a mistake to come back to the old surroundings, but her fame demanded it. The whole city waits to hear her next week at the Cirque des Bashibazoucks.

This morning she was tired from the journey; so, after my bath and a cup of coffee, I left her resting at the hotel and wandered into the old quarter.

I would not have dared to take her with me, even had she been able to go; and Gecko was away with some other friends, so I was alone. First I went to my old lodgings in the Rue Tire-Liard and then to the Rue des Saints Pères, where Trilby came to me. The room was vacant, and I went in and pictured her as she stood that night in the doorway. I wonder where she would have been now if she had not found me, or if some Honorable Colonel Desmond had been her protector. Now she sleeps well-cared for at the hotel, and shall never wander away again or be hungry or cold while I live to care for her. The studio in the Place St. Anatole des Arts was also vacant. It was stripped of every vestige of furnishing, and was vastly different from the bright and cheerful room of Christmas night of five years ago. I could have been good friends with its tenants if only circumstances had allowed. I wonder what has become of them. I can see Taffy and Little Billee yet splashing about in their tubs. Some of the habits of one's youth are hard to change; but, as for the comforts and luxuries of life, it is easy to accustom one's self to them when opportunity comes.

October 12th.

THE past five years were but the preparation for last night. It was the triumph of a lifetime, and well worth all the toil—all the privation—all the long years of waiting. Never before has such an audience greeted a singer. Not only Paris, but Germany, the provinces, London—all were there. Down near the front were the three tenants of the old studio. Ah, my friends! I could have welcomed even you most heartily if it had been safe. Perhaps some day we shall be able to understand each other better, and be good comrades, if only Trilby can forget. You see it was not all boasting. I tried to explain my aspirations, which were scarcely hopes, but could not. Is it not something to have gathered these people here from all countries? Is it not more to sway them as one will? And more—much more—to conciliate their good will so that they for a little time give up all their prejudices, and forget that they are French or English or whatever they may be, and that I am a Jew of Poland and cannot even speak so that they will fully understand me, except through the medium of my art? And Trilby—she sang as never before. I know not whether it was that her voice was sweeter, or because we were in more perfect sympathy. So that they might know that it was all she, and not the composer, I had her begin with "Au clair de la Lune," and all the glory was hers. It made no difference when she

sang the "Nussbaum"; it was her voice
that made them laugh or cry as we willed.
And then she sang "Ben Bolt" in English. I know not why I had selected
that song. I would not have chosen it
if I had known the audience we were to
have; but it was in the programme as I
had rehearsed it over and over again
with Trilby, and I did not dare to depart
from the order of the rehearsals. I
wonder if the three Englishmen down in
the front row remembered how she first
sang that song to us. No one laughs at
her singing now. Even Litolff would
not sneer as he compared her with
Mme. Alboni now. Well, messieurs,
that is but one little indication of a
change in her whole position which I
have wrought. If only she could have
realized it all herself, and rejoiced with
me in our triumph, my happiness would

have been complete. That cannot be—
at least not yet; but she shall have her
share of the benefits—yes, all! if they can
give her any pleasure.

October 13th.

I saw the three artists again to-day in the Place de la Concorde. With our English friends the appetite for the air of Bohemia does not last very long. It is not a congenial climate. They go back to their beer and skittles or port and fox-hunting—it is all the same—after a very short excursion into foreign realms. An Englishman is an Englishman before he is a citizen of any broader country. I wonder whether it is because they find their own ways so infinitely better than others, or because the routine of established customs is a safe shield behind which to hide.

I hardly knew the tenants of the studio in the Place St. Anatole des Arts, in their high hats and stiff frock-coats and collars that kept their necks from bending any way except straight to the right or left. The easy garb and manner of the days of the Latin Quarter are all gone. The big Taffy and the Scotch-Englishman do not grow old gracefully. It is in the blood. When youth and high spirits have gone, they are afraid to leave the beaten track. They are not interesting — these Englishmen — when they have passed their youth. The Scotch-Englishman carries his years the better; he seems to me as though he a little regretted the old days, and would go back if he could; but the other seems perfectly contented with the present; but neither of them is the man of five years ago. I wonder if they still get tipsy at night as in the old days; and if their fine dreams have all gone, just as their chivalry vanished the night Trilby disappeared. Well, my friends, I— Svengali—have, at least done what I purposed, although not exactly in the way I expected. Yet there is still one trouble: if only I were not so spent with the fight. One pays a high price for success, if he has to come all the way from the bottom. What if Trilby should have the old fancy return, and all my years of toil be as nothing! Will she? Ah, my little artist—I will see to it that it is not easy for you to renew the acquaintance. It is not the present I fear; but the memory that never dies in some natures.

October 14th.

THE applause last night was louder and longer than ever before. The enthusiasm was almost terrifying—it was like madness. I was forced to bring Trilby forward repeatedly. I could not let her sing again, for I feared it would be too much for her strength. As I kissed her hand and led her from the stage the last time, it all came over me like a torrent. What a pity, what a shame that this is not all as it seems— that she is not herself the artist singing with her heart as well as with her voice! To-day I heard a man say, "Think what she must have in her heart and brain only to sing like that!" She has it all in her heart and brain, but yet what they hear is not that, but only her voice guided by my heart and brain. Oh, if she could but once feel the glory of the power as the people hang upon her lightest note, and laugh or weep as they follow the music of her voice!

I could scarcely wait until we reached the hotel to try to make her follow of her own accord, as I played the music she had just sang. I urged her to try. She said, "Why do you ask me? You know I cannot sing, any more than I could in the old days at the studio; although, sometimes, I dream I can." Nevertheless, she did her best to please me. I too did all I could in the desperate hope of escaping from this position, which every day grows more intolerable. It was useless. At last she came and sat on the arm of my chair, and said; "I would do anything I could for you;

but I am afraid I can never learn to sing; and you—you poor dear—are foolish to waste your time on me." Then she spoke of the old days, and of Taffy and of McAllister and, last of all, of Little Billee—until I could bear it no longer, and seized her hand and covered it with kisses and cried, "Will you never forget that man? What has he done that you should carry his image forever and keep back from me some return for the constant and sincere love I have given you all these years?" She did.not answer for a time, but sat looking far away. Then she put her hand caressingly on my shoulder and said; "Come, let us watch the lights! How far down the street you can see them from this balcony —this is better than my old room in the Rue des Pousse-Cailloux. You must believe that I am thankful for all you have done for me; but do not let us talk of those things now."

So I am more than ever in torment, and wholly at a loss what to do. I cannot stop, and I dread to go on.

October 15th.

THE three artists are at a hotel near us. I am anxious, and cannot keep my thoughts away from them. To-day I saw them at dinner. They show the changes that have taken place in the past few years, even more at their table than in their walk and costume. Ah, messieurs! there has been too much of that Chartreuse and Rhum de la Jamaïque and Ratafia de Cassis, or those gills would not be so red and coarse nor the face so shiny. Be wary with that salad, Mr. Taffy. This is the time of life that marks the difference between the true artist and the Englishman.

.   .   .   .   .

With me also the early manner cannot die. What is born in us will persist even

after we think it is all forgotten.   I have
wandered about for hours, and am spent
with rage and shame and anger and
humiliation—and hate—hate—hate—for
the little artist who got without asking
what I gathered up and saved when he let
it fall, and now has come with his friends
to take it from me again; and I must
watch and watch and guard so that
Trilby, whom I have taught and worked
for and loved, does not even know that
they are here; for I feel, I know, that
all my work and love will be as nothing,
and Trilby will be gone, and I will be
alone again.   It makes me mad!   I am
crazy with apprehension!   To-day I met
the little artist in the post office of the
hotel, and all the rage and despair of
years blazed up.   I had not slept for
nights, planning that they should not
meet.   Why should they?   Had he kept

to her like a man when she loved him?
Had he found her cast out homeless in
the streets, and taken her in and cared
for her? Had he gone without, that she
might not feel privation; and invented
excuses, that she might not know that
what little he could give her was not
easily supplied? It was nothing—nothing but welcome, to me, that I should
have the chance to do it; but he had the
opportunity before all that, and let it
pass. And now why should he come to
spoil my last hope of happiness? He
has other friends at his home in England.
Can he not find someone among them to
please his mother and his uncle and all
his other relatives, and leave me her—my
only hope? Oh, Trilby! Trilby! If only
I were still young and not worn with
labor and privation! If only I too had
been always accustomed to the honors

and noble surroundings of life!   Then I
too could be calm and confident and easy
in my mind and bearing.   It all came to
me as I passed him; and, like a beast—
yes, like a dog from the mud of the
Ghettos—before I knew it, I had spat in
his face.   Would that I had struck him
or insulted him in any way but that, if I
must.   And then there was a struggle on
the stairs, and the big Taffy came, and
took his friend's part; and here, before
me, is his card; and I cannot finish the
quarrel as I would; for that would bring
it all to Trilby's ears, and she would
know that they are here, and then—oh!
If I only knew whether the old regard
for the little one is really strong enough
to take her from me!   Then I should
know what to do.

January 10th, 185-.

WE have been in London two days. Trilby is well, but pensive and distrait. I am fearful, and wish we had never left Germany. The constant effort is beginning to tell upon me. When one has been swimming alone so long, he needs a little support sometimes, even if it be but for a moment.

I saw the little artist on the street to-day. He is regarded as a great painter here. His painting, "The Moon Dial," is in the window at Moses Lyon's in Upper Conduit Street. Ah, Master Little Billee! it is easy to be great in one's own world, if you only pick out your world aright; but to compel unwilling

attention and win begrudged applause;
that is not the achievement of a dilettant
Englishman; that is the work of genius
and of a lifetime.

January 12th.

I WISH I knew whether Trilby is still really fond of the little artist or would care for him if they should meet again. Sometimes I try to consider that he has done me no wrong, except that Trilby loved him. Then again, I rage and am angry with him and with her and with all the world; and I walk up and down the streets for hours and hours and hours, until I am weak and exhausted; and then I come back to Trilby, and she is all sweetness, and I know she can never go back to the old life. How can she care for those who let her wander away alone? Now everyone is speaking of her, and the shop-windows are full of her photographs; but how would it have been if she had come to London as she left Paris with her little brother five years ago? But nevertheless, while it lasts, my head throbs, and all the old passions come back, and it is death to let this jealousy walk the streets with me so many nights.

January 15th.

I AM so broken with disgust and despair that I know not what to do. Ever since I met the little artist and his friend Taffy in Paris last October, I cannot sleep; or, if I doze, I awake in an agony of rage and shame. For days I have been half mad with apprehension and jealousy, fearing that she may meet him, or that the English speech may arouse all the old affection. I am not myself. It is because the struggle has been too hard and long, and I am failing. To-day during the rehearsal, I was short-tempered and irritable; and, in a moment of sudden anger, I struck Trilby with the little wand with which I lead. It was but a tap to draw her attention.

Gecko sprang upon me and struck me
with a small knife. He was right, and
yet no one need defend Trilby from me:
I would give my life for her. Yet he
was right; but, with what I was bearing
before, the little wound is too much, and
I am forbidden to lead for the present,
and so the opening concert must be post-
poned. Gecko, poor fellow! is pros-
trated with grief. I will be all right in a
few days. Of course Trilby cannot sing
without me, so, if I am not able to appear
very soon, I shall take my place in the
box nearest the stage and from there, I
think, I can control her voice—at least
we have arranged to try it.

January 16th.

I NEED not have feared for Trilby. She has not left my side for a moment. . . To-day I was allowed to attend a rehearsal. We tried the arrangement by which I am to lead from the box where Trilby can see me. It succeeds perfectly.

January 23d.

AND this is what I promised Trilby in the studio in the Place St. Anatole des Arts. I only half believed—no—I did not really believe it at all when I spoke. It was only a parable, a way of telling what I actually did hope, which was far less. The distance was too great; yet it is certain we are here. There will be no lack of Prinzessen, Comtessen, and Serene English Altessen there at the Drury Lane Theater to-night: but it is not the Prinzessen, Comtessen, or the Serene Altessen that I shall see. It is Trilby! Trilby! Trilby! and it is the music of her voice that I shall hear, and not the name "Svengali!" "Svengali!" It kills me that I do not know what she would feel and do if I should leave her to herself for a time. When this season is over, we will go to Prague or to Warsaw or Vienna, where the little artist cannot come, and there will be nothing to remind her of him or his friends, and we will rest and live with the people, and she shall learn that I can love without ambition. The music is good, and the gain and the applause—but—she, although she does not realize it, has worked hard and is tired, and my strength is almost gone. I must take care of myself if I am even to complete this engagement.

I did not guess that, after I had come all the way, I should discover that the goal was with me all the time. Ah, well—I had to take the whole journey to find it out. Still—it has been a very long way from Porlisz to London, and I am very tired to-night. How Marta would stare if she knew that I should almost prefer the little attic room in the old house in the Judenstrasse, and that worn red béret yonder that I wonder why I have kept, to the glare and applause of Drury Lane! It is not the horizontal distance that is hardest to travel. It is the ascent that leaves a man breathless and panting until, perhaps, he drops dead on the topmost step.

.　　　.　　　.　　　.　　　.

It is time to go to the theater. I must shake off this weakness and prepare. Yes, let it be "Svengali!" "Svengali!" "Svengali!" the people shout to-night. It will be as her name, not as mine, they will repeat it, and I am glad it is so. That is a longer way than the other, and I know not how I came it.

THE publication of the foregoing extracts from Svengali's diary has been especially desired by his friends in view of popular misconceptions of his character which have been caused by a work entitled "Trilby."

That book was written by Mr. George du Maurier, a friend of the English artist William Bagot, who is usually referred to by Mr. du Maurier, as well as by Svengali in the foregoing pages, as "Little Billee."

It will be readily understood that neither Mr. du Maurier's national preferences nor his friendship for Mr. Bagot would be likely to lead him to regard Svengali favorably; and, in spite of his desire to be just, this attitude is very plainly shown in his estimate of Svengali's character as given in " Trilby," as published by Harper & Brothers, pages 11 and 12 and 57 to 60: yet, even from this unfriendly source, we gather the following tributes to the character and genius of this remarkable man:

Page 62: "And then he set himself to teach her [Honorine] kindly and patiently at first."

Page 258: " He's an immense artist, and a great singing master."

Page 315: " Just as the clock struck, Svengali, in irreproachable evening dress, tall and stout and quite splendid in appearance, notwithstanding his long black mane (which had been curled), took his place at his desk. Our friends would have known him at a glance, in spite of the wonderful alteration time and prosperity had wrought in his outward man."

Page 324: Little Billee feels "A crushing sense of his own infinitesimal significance by the side of this glorious pair of artists, one of whom had been his friend and the other his love——"

Page 337: "And what must be her love for the man who had taught her and trained her, and revealed her towering genius to herself and to the world!—a man resplendent also, handsome and tall and commanding—a great artist from the crown of his head to the sole of his foot!"

Page 371: "He had for his wife, slave, and pupil, a fierce, jealous kind of affection that was a source of endless torment to him."

Page 387: Trilby says, "He was always very kind, poor Svengali. . . . He was kindness itself always."

Page 392: "He could be very funny, Svengali, though he *was* German, poor dear! . . . Poor Marta! Poor Gecko! What *will* they ever do without Svengali?"

Page 393: "I always had the best of everything. He insisted on that—even if he had to go without himself."

Page 428: Trilby did not remember when and where and by whom her trinkets were given her "Except a few that Svengali had given her himself, with many passionate expressions of his love, which seems to have been deep and constant and sincere."

Page 430: "At Trilby's request it was opened, and found to contain a large photograph, framed and glazed, of Svengali, in the military uniform of his own Hungarian band, and looking straight out of the picture, straight at you. He was standing at his desk, with his left hand turning over a leaf of music, and waving his baton with his right. It was a splendid photograph, by a Viennese photographer, and a most speaking likeness; and Svengali looked truly fine—all made up of importance and authority, and his big black eyes were full of stern command."

Page 432: "He was very handsome, I think; that uniform becomes him very well."

Page 452; Gecko says: "Svengali was the greatest artist I ever met! . . . He found me playing in the streets for copper coins, and took me by the hand, and was my only friend, and taught me all I ever knew."